Three Feet Under

A novel by

Paul Kropp

HIP-JR.

HIP Junior
Copyright © 2005 by High Interest Publishing

Library and Archives Canada Cataloguing in Publication

Kropp, Paul, 1948-
    Three feet under / Paul Kropp.

(HIP jr)
ISBN 1-897039-14-X

I. Title. II. Series.

PS8571.R772T47 2005   jC813'.54   C2005-905371-2

General editor: Paul Kropp
Text design and typesetting: Laura Brady
Illustrations drawn by: Matt Melanson
Cover design: Robert Corrigan

1 2 3 4 5 6 7   07 06 05 04 03 02

Printed and bound in Canada

High Interest Publishing is an imprint of the
Chestnut Publishing Group

Scott and Rico find a map to long-lost treasure. There's $250,000 buried in Bolton's mine. But then the school bully steals their map. When he heads for the old mine, the race is on.

CHAPTER 1

Maybe a Treasure Map

Scott and Rico walked down the alley. Maybe they should have looked around to see where they were. Instead, they talked about what Scott had found in his grandpa's attic.

"I found a map," Scott told his friend.

"Yeah, a treasure map," Rico said with a laugh. "So what else did you find? Like were there gold coins? Or maybe some old Wayne Gretzky cards?"

"My dad took all the sports cards," Scott said. "But I didn't let him see the map. I thought he'd

3

just throw it out. He threw out a lot of other stuff."

Scott had spent the weekend with his dad. They had cleaned up his grandpa's attic. His grandpa had died a month ago. Now the family was sorting out all his junk. For two days, Scott and his dad cleaned out a pile of stuff. There were old newspapers, books and records. There were old clothes, old computers and old TVs. These were worth nothing. Then there were old hockey and baseball cards — worth a lot.

Scott found the map inside a tin box. Mostly the box was full of stocks and bonds, but at the bottom was a map, a hand-drawn map. He gave the stocks and bonds to his dad. Scott put the map into his pocket.

"It might be a treasure map," Scott told his friend. "I'm not sure."

"So where is this map?" Rico asked.

"In my backpack," Scott replied. "I'll show you at recess."

Rico walked up on a curb edge. Of the two, he was the athlete. Rico was on all the school teams,

even though he was short. He had a big smile that all the kids liked. And he was cool, something that Scott would never be.

But Scott was smart. He read a book or two each night. His math was so good that the teachers asked him for answers. He could remember stuff for tests. He once learned all the battles of the War of 1812. Scott could do things like that.

The two of them had been friends all their lives. Their dads worked together. Their moms had coffee together. So the two kids had been friends since they were born. They were like brothers, but without the fights.

"Is it old?" Rico asked.

"What?"

"The map, you jerk!" Rico said. He didn't believe Scott, but still he wondered.

"Yeah, it's on old yellow paper," Scott replied.

"You think the map shows Bolton's treasure?" Rico asked.

Scott shrugged. "I don't know. It's just an old map, with some writing on it. But it shows the way down into the old mine on Mrs. Bolton's farm."

Bolton's treasure was famous in their town. A hundred years ago, a guy named Bolton robbed a bank and buried all the money. He got caught and went to jail, but died in there. The stolen money stayed buried — about $250,000 in old bills and coins. Lots of people had looked for it. But Bolton's treasure had never been found.

People figured that Bolton must have hidden the loot in the old mine. Bolton had been nearby when he was caught. His aunt owned the mine. But the old coal mine spread for miles. It was deep, dark and wet. There were just too many places where the treasure might have been hidden. People had dug holes and followed tips. Once they had even brought in a bulldozer. Still, the money was never found.

"You know what I think?" Scott asked.

Rico didn't find out. Before Scott could say another word, they were in trouble.

In front of them was a kid named Clay Prentice. He was the biggest, meanest kid in school. Behind them was a bully from grade 7. On one side was Clay's older brother. On the fourth side was a fence. They were trapped.

"Time to pay up, boys," Clay told them. "A loonie each to use this alley."

"It's not your alley, Clay!" Rico snapped back.

"Yeah, but that's what we charge," Clay replied. "Pay up or get hurt — your choice."

The boys had been caught like this before. The last time they paid, but it was only a quarter. This time, they didn't even have that much.

One guy kept moving up from the back. Clay's brother was moving in from the side. Clay just stood in front and laughed at them.

"We don't have any money," Scott told them. *Don't cry,* he told himself. Whatever you do, don't let them see you cry.

"Then we get to have some fun," Clay told them. "Get 'em!" he shouted.

The three bullies jumped on them at the same time. The odds weren't fair — three against two. Clay landed a punch right into Scott's gut. Scott screamed.

But Rico kicked. He was faster than these guys.
He kicked Clay's brother right where it hurts the
most. The guy bent over in pain, and Rico saw a
way out.

"Run!" he shouted to Scott.

But Scott couldn't run. He had two guys on him
now. Clay was grabbing at his backpack. The older

kid was holding his head. Scott was struggling, but he was trapped.

So Rico ran back and pulled the one bully off his friend. Then he grabbed his friend's arm and pulled him free.

RRRIPPP! One strap on Scott's backpack ripped.

"My backpack!" Scott yelled.

"Let it go!" Rico yelled.

Scott pulled his arm free of the backpack and took off. When they were a block away, they looked back. There were Clay and his gang, going through Scott's backpack.

"Kiss your lunch goodbye," Rico said.

"My lunch is nothing," Scott told him. "But my grandpa's map is in there."

Rico just shook his head. "Don't worry. Clay will take your lunch and your money, but he's too stupid to steal a map."

CHAPTER 2

Not That Stupid

The two boys had to take a back route to school. By the time they got to the playground, most of the other kids had gone in. The three bullies were nowhere in sight. But Scott's ripped backpack was right by the fire door. His books were on the ground. His notebook was in a puddle. His homework was blowing in the wind.

And the backpack was empty!

"They got the map," Scott said.

Rico swore, then looked through the backpack again. Nothing.

"I guess Clay isn't that stupid," Rico said. "Come on. I'll help pick up your homework from the fence."

They could have told their principal what happened. They could have gone to the office and explained it all. Scott had been robbed — that was the simple truth. The gang had taken his MP3 player, a Lego truck and his lunch.

But *telling* wasn't what kids did. If you told on Clay or his brother, they'd get you back. There were stories about that.

"We're going to get even," Rico told his friend at recess.

"Yeah, how?" Scott asked.

Scott was bent over, holding his stomach. It hurt, and so did his shoulder.

"We'll go get the map back," Rico said brightly. "I'll get a couple of guys and we'll take them on. We'll make it five against three, or ten against three."

"Really?"

"Yeah," Rico replied. "You know what they say —
there's strength in numbers. Those guys stole your
MP3 player and the map. You should get them
both back."

"You're right," Scott said. The idea cheered him
up. "That stuff is mine!"

The boys went around to their friends, and they
had many of them. Some of the guys were scared
off by Clay and his gang, but not all. By the end
of lunch, they had eight guys ready. Right after

school, they'd follow Clay and get the stuff back.

It was a perfect plan. The guys were solid. They could force Clay to give the map back. It was time for the decent kids to fight back. Too much lunch money was going to Clay's gang. Somehow it had to stop.

The problem with perfect plans is that they mess up. Last class in the day was science. Rico and Scott looked around the science lab. Their friends were there and ready. They gave each other the thumbs up.

"But where's Clay?" Rico asked Scott.

"Clay Prentice?" asked the science teacher. "Where's Clay?"

No one said a word. The truth was simple — Clay had skipped out.

Only Rico and Scott could guess the reason why.

"So now what do we do?" Scott asked as they left the school. Their group of eight guys was ready, but the Prentice brothers weren't there.

"Wait till tomorrow?" Rico replied.

"Yeah, great," Scott told him. The other kids

had left, and now they walked down the street alone. "The map will be long gone by then. I bet that Clay is out there digging right now."

They walked in silence for a while. It was cold for spring, cold and wet. After the day so far, they both felt lousy. But then Rico had an idea.

"You looked at the map, right?" he asked.

"Yeah, a couple of times," Scott replied.

"So you must remember some of it," Rico went on.

"Yeah, I guess . . . some of it."

"So that's the answer," Rico declared. "You'll just have to remember the map. Then we use your memory to draw it over, and we follow the map in your head."

Scott turned to look at his friend. Sometimes he thought that Rico was crazy. This was one of those times.

"Yeah, and then?"

"Then we go into the mine," Rico told him, "and find the treasure." Rico was smiling now, the crazy grin that always got them in trouble.

"And when do we do this?" Scott asked.

"In about half an hour," Rico told him. "I just have to tell my mom that I'm having dinner at your house and you . . ."

"Tell my mom that I'm having dinner at yours," Scott replied.

CHAPTER 3

Into the Mine

The two lies worked. Both boys could get away until eight o'clock. Rico went to his shed and got a shovel. Scott went to his house and got two flashlights. They put on some warm clothes and met at their clubhouse. The clubhouse was just a few sheets of plywood against a tree, but it was their place. "All others keep out!" read the sign. No others had ever tried to get in, but that didn't matter.

"Okay, remember the map. Think hard!" Rico

said. He gave Scott a piece of paper and a pencil. "You got it?"

"Not so fast," Scott replied. He closed his eyes and tried to see the map in his mind. *One tunnel, no three, then the split, then . . .*

Scott began to draw on the piece of paper. He had only looked at the map three times. Still, most of the map was coming back to him.

"That's good," Rico said as his friend drew. "Now where's the treasure?"

Scott closed his eyes and tried to think. The real map did not have an X on it but a kind of circle with some words. The words came back to him — *three feet under.* But where was the circle?

"You got it!" Rico yelled when Scott put an X on his map. "You're a genius."

"I'm not sure I got it right," Scott told him.

"You'll remember the rest when we get there," Rico replied. "Let's get going."

The entrance to the mine was an hour from their houses. The boys had to ride their bikes over

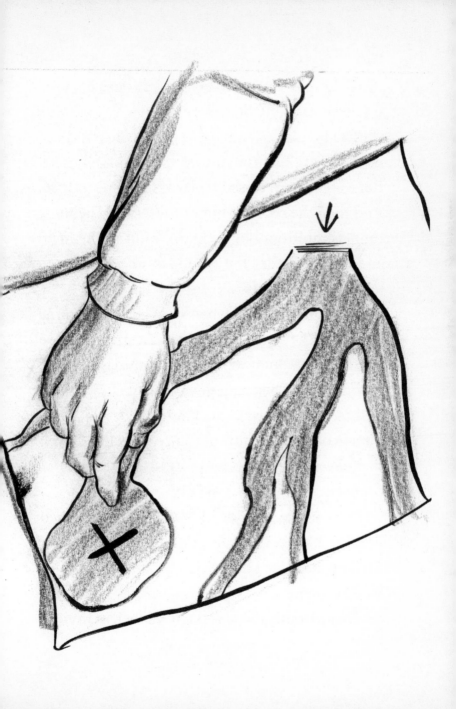

the old mine tunnels to get there. These days, no one ever went into the old mine.

The Bolton coal mine had been a big one. Back in the 1920s, half the men in town worked there. But a big cave-in closed much of the mine in 1926. And then the coal ran out in the 1950s. The mine tunnels ran from Bolton's farm right to the town — and well under the town. No wonder no one had found the treasure.

It was five o'clock when they got to the mine entrance. The sun, if the sky were clear, would have started to set. But it was a wet, cloudy day, so there was no sun. They hid their bikes behind some bushes, then walked to the mine.

Of course, the mine entrance was closed over. There were big signs: MINE CLOSED. KEEP OUT! DANGER!

"Looks like they don't want us inside," Rico joked.

"Looks like somebody else has already gone in," Scott replied.

They saw that the big concrete block in front of

the mine entrance had been pulled away. Now there was enough room for both of them to squeeze inside. They were not the first kids to have done so. And they had a hunch who had gone in just before them.

"What do we do if we come across Clay Prentice?" Scott asked.

"Hit him with a shovel," Rico replied.

"No, really," Scott said. "Do we run, or talk to him, or work together?"

"Yeah, Clay is real big on teamwork," Rico said, making fun of Scott. "I say we figure that out if we see him. Play it by ear, as my dad says."

Rico got a lot of old phrases from his dad. Sometimes they were good. *Strength in numbers* — now that made sense. *Play it by ear,* well, that could mean anything.

"Okay, now I've got the really big question. Are you sure you want to do this?" Scott asked.

"Of course I'm sure," Rico said. "Clay is going to walk out of here with a fortune, all thanks to your map. It should be yours, not his."

"Yeah, I guess," Scott sighed. He looked at the DANGER and KEEP OUT signs.

Scott was worried. He had never been in a mine before. He'd heard about cave-ins and coal gas and miners getting killed. He knew that mines were dangerous. He wondered if they were ready to go down. They had two flashlights in his backpack. Rico had a water bottle and two candy bars. They had on their winter coats. But if they got trapped or lost, they'd be in big trouble.

"You sure you want to do this?" Scott asked.

"Don't act like a wuss," Rico told him. He could see the fear in Scott's eyes. "If Clay can do this, we can do it. Let's go!"

CHAPTER 4

Dark and Darker

The Bolton mine was dark and cold. Three steps inside and the boys could see their breath. Six steps and Scott put on his hat. Nine steps and they needed flashlights to see. A dozen steps and they couldn't see the entrance.

"I don't like this," Scott whispered.

"Don't be a wuss," Rico repeated.

"How do we find our way back?" Scott asked.

"We, uh . . . well, there's only one tunnel."

"Until it splits into three."

"Then we'll play it by ear," Rico told him. "Now keep quiet. I'm pretty sure Clay Prentice is in here someplace."

Scott was afraid outside the mine. Now his fear was even worse. They should have brought some way to mark the path. They should have brought bigger flashlights. They should have brought warmer clothes. Scott did not know a mine would be so dark. Or so cold. Or so wet. Each breath made a cloud of steam in the cold air.

The Bolton mine was an old one. These days, mines have big shafts and tunnels. They have lights and fans and clean air. The miners go down in cars and use big machines to get the coal. But the Bolton mine had none of that. The top was held up by wood beams, not steel. There were no lights. The air smelled like wet, rotting dirt.

Scott would not have gone down, not on his own. But Rico just pushed ahead. If Rico was afraid, he did not let it show.

The roof of the mine was so low that both boys had to crouch. They walked like old men, with their heads down. Water on the floor soaked their feet.

"How far do we have to go?" Scott asked.

"Not sure," Rico said. "Your map wasn't *to scale*, you know."

"Yeah, but we've been under for quite a while."

Rico pushed the button on his watch. "More like ten minutes."

Scott said no more. He was scared, cold and hungry. But he let Rico lead on. What choice did he have? Turn around and go back by himself? Rico would never let him live it down.

"Look," Rico whispered after a few more minutes. "This is where the tunnel splits in three. Which way do we go?"

Scott tried to remember. An hour ago, he had drawn a map. Now his mind was a blank.

"Uh, left, I think," Scott replied. He could have pulled his map from his pocket, but he didn't check it.

Rico led the way. The tunnel on the left wasn't as wide as the first one. The roof was a little bit lower. The air was a little bit colder.

They walked for another ten minutes. Then Rico stopped them.

"I don't think this is right," he said.

"Why not?" Scott asked.

"We should be in a big room," Rico replied. "That's what you drew on your map. It made sense, too. The miners would dig for coal in the big rooms. Then the ponies would take it out the tunnels. Remember that book we read?"

Scott wasn't thinking about a book. His problem was right in front of him. "So we're lost?" Scott asked.

A sudden bolt of fear shot to his heart. They were way underground. No one knew they were here. Scott's map might be all wrong. It was cold and dark and scary, and now they were lost. Scott felt like crying or screaming for help.

"No, we just have to go back," Rico told him. "Where's that map of yours?"

Scott handed the map to his friend. He saw his hand trembling as it held the paper.

"You scared?" Rico asked.

"No," Scott lied. "Just freezing."

Rico looked down at the map while Scott pointed one flashlight at it. Then Rico shook his head.

"You dork!" he declared. "Can't you tell your right from your left?"

"Yeah, sure I can."

"Well, I doubt it," Rico shot back. "We should have taken the *right*-hand tunnel. This one doesn't go anywhere."

Scott felt ashamed. He should have checked his own map. Now they had wasted ten minutes — and would waste another ten minutes going back.

"Come on," Rico said, disgusted. He turned quickly and knocked into his friend's hand. Scott was holding the flashlight in that hand. In a

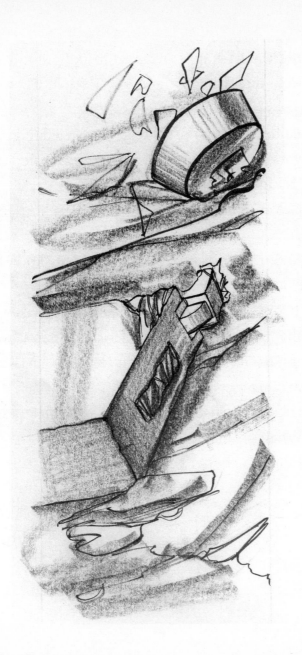

second, the flashlight smashed to the ground —
and went out.

Rico swore.

Scott picked up the flashlight and tried to get it
going. He popped out the batteries and twisted the
lens. No luck. It was dead.

"Great," Rico said. "Now we've got just one
light."

"And if yours goes out," Scott added, "we're in
real trouble."

There was a moment of silence. In the dark, wet
air, the boys looked at each other. Scott was
shaking from the cold or from fear or both. Rico
was shaking too, breathing hard.

"You know what I think?" Rico said at last.

"What?"

"I think we better get out of here, like fast."

CHAPTER 5

Messed Up

Fear is not a good thing. When a person is afraid, things go wrong. When a person is afraid, he makes mistakes. When a person is afraid, little mistakes become big ones.

Both Scott and Rico were afraid now.

The tunnel seemed much darker with only one flashlight. Even worse, that light seemed to be getting dimmer.

With two lights, they could see the walls and follow the tunnel. With one light, they could only see the tunnel floor. It was shiny and wet, with cracks and lumps that could make a person fall.

The boys were moving too fast now. The fear had crept into their bones and was taking over. It pushed them to rush ahead, to make mistakes.

"Sheesh," Scott yelled.

Rico turned back and saw his friend down on the tunnel floor. Scott was on his hands and knees, soaked.

Rico held out a hand to help his friend up.

"I don't get it," Rico said.

"Get what?"

"We should be back where the tunnel split in three, but we're not."

"Maybe it's just up ahead," Scott replied. Now he was the one trying to be cheerful. He was the one pretending that he wasn't scared.

"Yeah, maybe," Rico replied. But his voice was high and shaky.

They pushed forward into the dark.

Scott thought about home. If he weren't down here, he would be eating dinner. His dad did the cooking, and mostly it was bad. Dinner would be burned or undercooked. It would be noisy from the TV and his baby sister screaming. But it would be home. It would be warm and bright and cozy.

It wouldn't be a mine tunnel way under the ground.

Rico thought about the flashlight and the map. If Scott's map was right, they should be at the main tunnel. But Scott only *remembered* the map. Maybe he remembered it wrong. Or maybe the old map was wrong. It was just a hand-drawn map from an old guy's attic. There must be other tunnels and shafts not on the map.

Rico saw his flashlight getting dimmer. It was a big, waterproof flashlight. Scott's dad used it to work on their old boat. The battery was supposed to be good for three hours. But was it fresh when they started? They had been in the mine for an hour now, but the light was less than half as strong.

What if he dropped it? Then they'd be blind as well as lost.

Then they'd be dead.

Maybe that thought made Rico trip. His right foot hit a ledge. His left foot kept moving. And suddenly Rico was falling forward. He tried to catch himself, but it didn't help. *Hold on to the flashlight,* he told himself.

Rico and the flashlight hit the floor at the same time. Rico was fine.

But the flashlight was smashed.

"Sheesh!" Rico cried out. Then he added a few choice words. All the words made an echo in the dark tunnel.

The tunnel was as dark as a tomb. It was so dark, Rico saw little sparks of light in his eyes. But the sparks were *in* his eyes, not outside. There was no light in the tunnel itself.

"Rico, where are you?" Scott cried out.

"Here," Rico said, getting up from the floor.

In the dark, the two moved towards each other's voices. In a second, they bumped shoulders.

"I messed up," Rico told his friend. "Sorry."

"We both messed up," Scott replied. "Now we're even."

34

In the darkness, there was nothing. The boys could hear each other. They could feel the heavy coats they wore. They could feel the cold stone beneath them. But they couldn't see a thing.

"You got any idea what we should do?" Scott asked.

"Nope," Rico replied. "I think we're toast, buddy."

There was a bit of silence while they let that sink in. The air did not move. All they could hear was dripping water.

"When we don't get back," Scott said, "our parents will start a search. They'll find our bikes."

"Yeah, in the morning," Rico replied. "Maybe."

"So we just have to stay put until then," Scott said. Now he was the strong one. He was the one who held on to hope.

"Yeah, sure," Rico said.

"I've got a couple of candy bars," Scott replied. The lower Rico sank, the more Scott tried to cheer him up.

"Yeah, like we really deserve a treat."

Scott ignored him. He felt into his backpack and found the candy bars. Carefully, he pulled them out.

"Here — a Mars bar," he said. He pushed the candy bar where Rico's hand should be.

Scott waited for his friend to take the bar. He waited for his friend to say "thanks" or something. But Rico couldn't speak. He was too busy crying.

CHAPTER 6

Sounds in the Darkness

The boys sat in the dark, eating their candy bars. This just made Scott thirsty. He had a bottle of water and almost opened it. *But we might need this,* he said to himself. If they were going to spend a whole night in the mine, they'd need water.

They would also need warmer jackets. The cold in the mine seeped into their bones. It was damp. Their feet were wet. The air was freezing.

"You know what I think?" Scott asked.

"What?"

"I think it's going to be a long cold night."

"Yeah," Rico replied. He pounded his arms, trying to make his blood run faster. Then he had an idea. "You still have that little light on your keychain?"

The simple truth came like a slap. "Yeah," Scott replied. He reached into his pocket, pulled out his keys, and there was the light. He flicked it on.

It wasn't much light in the dark tunnel. It barely lit up their faces and hands. But it was better than total darkness.

"Okay, turn it off," Rico ordered. "That's all the light we have. We'd better save it, just in case."

"So you think we should just sit here?" Scott asked.

"Yeah," Rico told him. "I think we're dead lost. I think your map missed a couple of things. And I think we should have marked our way back out. Pretty stupid, eh?"

Scott sighed. It *was* pretty stupid. They hadn't been ready to go into the mine. They didn't have a

plan in case they got lost. They'd been stupid.

So they sat on a stone ledge, staring into blackness. In the distance, they could hear water dripping. Sometimes there was the sound of wings. *Bats*, Scott thought, and began to shake.

"What time is it?" Scott asked.

Rico pushed the button on his watch. Seven thirty.

"We're missing *Family Guy*," Scott said.

"Yeah," Rico agreed. "And we're missing dinner, too. Which do you miss more?"

"*Family Guy*," Scott replied. "My dad can't cook to save his life."

Again the two boys fell into silence. The gloom was too much, the damp air too cold. They tried to act like they'd be found in the morning, but both of them knew that the odds were lousy. They might be down here for days. They might die, lost in Bolton's mine.

Chunk — chunk — chunk.

"What's that?" Scott asked.

"Could be my stomach," Rico told him. "I'm starving."

"No, listen . . ."

Chunk — chunk — chunk.

"It sounds like digging," Rico whispered.

"Do you think it's . . ."

"Shhh!"

For the first time in an hour, the boys felt hope. There was someone else down in the mine. There was someone — not too far away — digging.

"It's got to be Clay!" Scott blurted out.

"Shhh!" Rico repeated.

41

Scott turned on his keychain flashlight. Then both boys got to their feet and began to move toward the sound.

They moved slowly. It was hard to see the tunnel floor and hard to follow the sound. The *chunk-chunk-chunk* came like an echo from all sides. But soon the boys found the spot where the three tunnels split off. They had a choice.

"Hey, we can get out of here," Scott said.

"Or we can stop Clay from stealing the treasure," Rico replied.

In the darkness, they had to choose. Turn right, run out and reach the warm night air. Turn left, follow the tunnel and deal with Clay. For a second, the choice hung between them. It was like a question waiting for an answer.

They made up their minds at the same moment.

"Let's go see what he found," Rico said.

"I'm right behind you," Scott agreed.

The two boys turned left. Now they had to be very quiet. The *chunk-chunk-chunk* was getting louder. Scott knew from the map that they were only a short way from the treasure. Only a short way from Clay Prentice.

They kept moving forward. Sometimes they'd bump into each other, but they said nothing. At last, in the distance, they saw a light. Scott flipped off his tiny flashlight. They walked slowly toward the light at the end of the tunnel.

When they got to the end, they saw him. Clay was in the first big mining room. He had two lights aimed at the stones, and he was digging. There was sweat dripping off his forehead. His hands were covered with dirt.

Chunk-chunk-clang!

Clay's shovel had hit something. He began digging faster. More and more dirt came out and up. It made a little pile beside Clay on the mine floor.

"Got it!" Clay said, talking to himself.

He pushed the shovel down into the hole. Then he leaned hard on the shovel handle. Nothing happened. Clay swore and began digging more dirt.

Scott wanted to say something. He wanted to tell Rico that Clay had found the treasure. But he couldn't speak. One word and Clay would know they were there.

Clay pushed the shovel down again, leaning hard on the handle. Something began to lift up from the hole. Clay bent over and pulled at something heavy. At first, it still seemed stuck in the ground. But then something came free.

In a few seconds, an old metal chest was on the floor of the mine. Clay picked up one of his lights and looked closely. There was an old lock on one side that held it closed.

Clay picked up the shovel and stuck the tip into the lock. Then he pulled back on the handle until the lock snapped.

Scott and Rico held their breath as Clay opened the box.

"Well, look at that!" Clay said out loud.

CHAPTER 7

Finders Keepers

From where they stood, Rico and Scott couldn't see much. Their eyes were used to the dark, but they were at a bad angle to see much. Clay was bent over a big, old, metal box. He reached inside and pulled out something.

When Clay lifted his hands, the boys knew. He was holding money — a big handful of money.

"Looks like I hit the jackpot," Clay said. Then he began laughing. They were great big laughs, real whoops of joy.

It was more than Scott could stand. He took a few steps out from the darkness. Then he spoke up, "That's my grandpa's money!"

For a second, Clay was stunned. He thought he was alone in the mine. Now there was a voice coming from the darkness.

"Who . . . who's there?" Clay cried. His voice was up high, scared. Quickly he grabbed a light and aimed it into the dark.

For a moment, the two boys just stared at each other. Scott stared into the light. Clay stood still, his mouth dropping open.

"You stole my grandpa's map," Scott went on. "That money belongs to him . . . or to me."

"Yeah, right!" Clay mocked him. "Finders keepers. And who says that I stole the old man's map? It's your word against mine, Scott."

That's when Rico stepped out of the shadows. He smiled at Clay, as if he were in control of the whole thing.

"And my word, too," Rico added. "I bet that money really belongs to the bank. But we should all get some kind of reward. Now if you stop being a jerk, maybe we'll cut you in for a share."

"Fat chance, loser," Clay told him. "My share is 100 percent. Your share is zero. Now I think you two should get out of here. I've got a treasure to take home."

The three boys stared at one another. If it came to a fight, it would be two against one. But Clay was bigger than either Rico or Scott. He was used to beating up kids, and he knew how to use his fists. Scott would be useless in a fight. So the odds weren't that good, and Rico knew it. He decided to bluff.

"Over my dead body," Rico said.

"If that's what you want," Clay snapped back. He grabbed the shovel and began walking towards Rico.

"What are you going to do?" Rico asked. "Hit me?"

"Yeah, for a start," Clay replied. He held the shovel in two hands, moving forward.

Rico didn't like these odds. He moved back,

away from Clay, into the darkness. With his dark coat and muddy pants, Rico couldn't be seen.

Scott was really scared. He had never won a fight in his life. Now a big kid was coming at him with a shovel. He made a quick choice.

He ran!

"I'm going to get you," Clay swore. But Clay had a problem, too. He couldn't hold both the shovel and a flashlight. To see, he needed the light. To fight, he needed the shovel. Quickly, he made his choice. Clay raced into the darkness, swinging the shovel back and forth.

By now, Scott was back at the tunnel entrance. He could see Clay's shadow but knew that Clay couldn't see him.

But Rico was still trapped in the mine. He was there, somewhere, in the dark. Sooner or later, Clay would find him.

Rico took that moment to make fun of Clay. "Over here, reject!" Rico called.

Scott heard the voice, then saw Clay stomping over to the right. There was a crash. Clay had smashed the shovel into a wall.

There was a clatter of feet, and then Rico spoke again. "Missed me!"

Clay moved to the left, further down the mine room. It was pitch black down there, but he must have seen a shape. SMASH. Clay slammed the shovel into something.

Please don't let that be Rico, Scott prayed.

It wasn't. From another spot, Scott and Clay heard Rico laugh. "Missed me again."

Scott was amazed. His friend was playing cat-and-mouse with this bully. But Clay had a shovel, and he was a lot bigger than either of them. Rico wouldn't have a hope if Clay found him.

Clay went back to his flashlight and beamed it all over. He found Rico in one corner. "I can see you now," Clay declared. He grabbed the shovel, then began running right towards Rico. "Now I've got you!"

Clay lifted the shovel to one side, than swung it like a baseball bat. SMASH. There was the sound of metal hitting something. If he hit Rico like that, Rico would be out cold.

But Clay hadn't hit Rico. He'd smashed the shovel into an old wood beam. The beam held up the roof of the mine. There was a cracking sound . . . then a creaking sound . . .

"Nice work, reject," Rico called out.

But Clay said nothing. All three of them could hear a strange sound all around them. It was a sound of splintering wood and shaking earth. Suddenly, there was coal dust falling from the roof. Even the floor seemed to be shaking.

Clay had knocked down a support beam. Now the roof was coming down!

In a second, Rico came running to the mouth of the tunnel. He grabbed Clay's flashlight so they could see their way.

"Let's get out of here!" he screamed.

In a flash, Scott was right behind him. The two boys ran like crazy. Behind them, the roof of the mine was coming down in huge pieces.

CHAPTER 8

A Tough Choice

In a few minutes, Scott and Rico had reached the mine entrance. They crawled into the dark night outside, then tried to catch their breath.

The mine had collapsed behind them as they ran. A cloud of dust and coal gas had covered them. Now both boys were black from soot. They were coughing, tired and beaten. But they were alive.

"Made it," Rico said. Then he broke into coughs.

"Yeah . . . just," Scott agreed. "For a while it was looking, like, bad."

"Yeah, but we're okay," Rico said.

"What about Clay?"

"Ask me if I care," Rico snapped back. "That guy tried to kill me."

"Yeah, but he's still in there," Scott replied. "And we'd be in there too if it wasn't for his flashlight."

The two boys looked at each other. A cloud of dust was coming out of the mine entrance, but there was no sign of Clay. They had to decide — go home or go back in. The decision did not take long.

"Okay, so I'm an idiot," Rico said.

"Me too," Scott added.

With that, Rico grabbed the flashlight and led the way back into the mine.

"Clay!" Scott screamed out. Then the dust got in his throat and he began to cough.

"Clay — this way!" Rico called.

But there was no answer. With all the dust, they could hardly see at all. The flashlight beam showed dust, but only a short distance. Beyond that, there was nothing.

"Clay!"

Silence.

The boys kept moving into the mine. The dust made it hard to breathe. Scott began to cough like crazy. He put his sleeve up in front of his mouth and nose, like an air filter. Rico did the same.

"Clay!"

In the distance was a sound, a sound like a voice. It was hard to hear, as if the voice were buried deep inside the mine.

"Clay, is that you?" Rico yelled.

Again, a sound. As the boys moved on, the sound became louder. It was like screaming or crying.

"Clay, we're coming!" Scott yelled.

Now they could hear words. "Help! I need help!"

In a few minutes, they knew why. In front of them was a wall of rock and loose stone. It blocked the path of the tunnel.

"Clay, are you in there?" Rico yelled.

"Yeah," came the reply. "I can see your light."

The two boys looked at each other. If Clay could see their light, there had to be an opening in the rock wall. But they couldn't see any hole in the rocks. There was too much dust and smoke.

"We'll go to the farmhouse and call for help," Scott yelled.

"No, don't leave me here," Clay begged. "I brought the treasure box this far. I'll share it with you."

Rico shook his head. No wonder Clay was stuck in the mine — he'd dragged the money while Scott and Clay were running. It must have slowed him down a lot.

Scott figured it was not the time to talk about sharing treasure. The problem was getting out alive. Most of the mine had caved in. There was no telling how long this tunnel would stay clear.

Rico began moving the light over the wall of rock. "Tell me when it seems really bright," he shouted.

From his side of the wall, Clay stared at a pile of dark stones. On the other side were Scott and Rico and freedom. On his side was a box with a quarter of a million dollars.

"Okay . . . the light is shining right in," Clay told them. "I'll stick my arm through the hole."

From the outside, Rico and Clay stared at the other side of the same wall. Suddenly, they saw a muddy hand wiggling between two stones. The opening was small. It was barely big enough for Clay's arm.

"Okay, we see you," Rico called out. "Get your arm out and we'll pull away some rocks."

Both boys got on their knees in front of the rock wall. Rico pulled at a big rock near the opening. But it wouldn't move. Scott pulled away some smaller stones beneath the opening. Soon he had made the hole twice as large as it was. But there was still no way that Clay could fit through it.

"See the big rock," Rico said. "If we both pull . . ."

Scott began to cough again. When he stopped, they both grabbed at the large rock and tried to move it.

"On the count of three," Rico said. "One . . . two . . . Pull!"

Pulling with all their strength, they slid the rock halfway out, then turned it sideways.

"The hole is big enough," Scott declared. "If we pull it all the way, the whole wall could collapse."

"C'mon, Clay, you can squeeze through that!" Rico said.

"Yeah, but the box won't go through," Clay called back.

"Leave the box!" Scott cried, then he began coughing again.

"Clay, you can stay in there with the money, and wait for help, or you can squeeze through," Rico told him. "We've already risked our necks to come back in here. We're not going to get killed so you can get rich. Now make up your mind. In twenty seconds, we're out of here."

Rico was like that. Once he made up his mind, there was no fooling around.

"Five seconds left," Rico shouted.

When the time was up, there was nothing more to say. "Okay, Scott, let's go," Rico said. "Clay, we'll call for help when we get up on top."

Clay was scared stiff. He was trapped in a collapsed mine. It was dark, cold and wet. It could be hours before anyone came down to rescue him. He wanted the money, all right. He had pictured all the stuff he would buy. In his mind, he was already rich. But what good would it do him if he was dead?

"Wait!" Clay screamed in a high voice. "I'm coming."

In a second, Scott and Rico saw Clay's head

sticking out. Then his shoulders got stuck, so Clay had to pull back and take off his coat. On the second try, Clay got both his head and shoulders through the opening. Then the two boys grabbed his arms and pulled the rest of his body through.

Clay fell to the tunnel floor, just as the large rock in the wall twisted free.

From inside the mine, there was a deep, rumbling sound.

"Let's get out of here!" Rico cried.

CHAPTER 9

All That Is Buried

The three boys ran like crazy as the tunnel fell down behind them. A rush of dust and foul air came at their backs. But soon they were climbing out of the mine.

Behind them came a blast of dust and cold air. The ground beneath their feet shook. Bolton's mine collapsed with a deep boom.

Rico, Scott and Clay looked at one another. For a moment, they thought about the last few hours. They thought about how close they had come to dying. They thought about how they had fought underground.

But they said nothing. Without a word, they grabbed their bikes and rode home.

* * *

Old Mrs. Bolton felt the mine cave in. She called the police, who came out at ten o'clock. They found that the mine entrance was blocked with stones. Mrs. Bolton and the police were pleased. The old Bolton mine had been a pain for them. Teenagers would sneak in. Treasure hunters would go digging. Sooner or later, someone would get killed. Mrs. Bolton worried about that.

Now there was no Bolton mine. It was history.

For a few weeks, the three boys kept their mouths shut. Clay was the first to tell the story. He told his brother that he found the treasure. He told his brother that he had been trapped in the mine. He said that he had to leave the treasure behind.

His brother just laughed.

Today, there are rumors in the town. There are old rumors about the Bolton treasure. There are new rumors that some kids found the treasure. There's even a rumor that some kids are buried in the mine.

Some of those rumors are true. But only three people know for sure.

One of them is Clay Prentice. He stopped beating up on little kids. He stopped stealing lunch money. Clay Prentice never became a good guy, but he stopped being a bully.

Rico kept thinking about the money that he and Scott almost found. He thought about what the money could have bought. But then he remembered what it was like to be trapped in the mine. No box of money was worth that.

Scott went on to write a story about the mine and its treasure. In his story, the kids got out with the money. They bought great cars and cool TVs. They went on trips to France and Mexico. They were heroes.

"I showed the story to Mrs. Rad," Scott told

Rico. The two boys were at the clubhouse after school. Mrs. Rad was the nickname for their new teacher. She was doing a writing workshop in class.

"She like it?" Rico asked him.

"Yeah," Scott replied. "Except for the end. The part where the two guys get all the money."

"What's wrong with that?"

Scott just shrugged. "Mrs. Rad said she didn't believe it."

Bats Past Midnight

by SHARON JENNINGS

Sam and Simon wonder about a fancy car that hangs around their school late at night. When they try to find out more, they end up in trouble at school, at home and with the police.

Choose Your Bully

by LORI JAMISON

Sam and Richard have a great idea to deal with their school bully — hire a bodyguard. But when their bodyguard starts to bully them, they have to get smarter.

The Crash

by PAUL KROPP

A school bus slides off a cliff in a snowstorm. The bus driver is out cold. One of the guys is badly hurt. Can Craig, Rory and Lerch find help in time?

Paul Kropp is the author of more than fifty novels for young people. His work includes nine award-winning young adult novels, many high-interest novels, as well as books and stories for both adults and early readers.

Paul Kropp's best-known novels for young adults, *Moonkid and Liberty* and *Moonkid and Prometheus*, have been translated into many languages and have won awards around the world. His illustrated books for younger readers include *What a Story!* and four books based on Mr. Dressup characters. His high-interest novels have sold nearly a million copies in Canada and the United States. For more information on Paul, visit his website at www.paulkropp.com.